Bumper Tubbs

Bumper Tubbs

Written and Illustrated by
DAVID McPHAIL

HOUGHTON MIFFLIN COMPANY BOSTON / 1980

For Arthur, the one and only

Library of Congress Cataloging in Publication Data

McPahail, David M.
    Bumper Tubbs.

    SUMMARY: The adventures of an alligator who turns
mishaps into successes with luck and help from his
friends.
    [1. Alligators – Fiction.   2. Friendship – Fiction.
3. Animals – Fiction]   I. Title.
PZ7.M2427Bu   [E]   79-26360
ISBN 0-395-28477-5

The Stories

The Sunrise

BUMPER TUBBS lives in a little cottage near the ocean. In front of the cottage is a small yard, and around the yard is a white picket fence with roses climbing all over it.

Beside Bumper's cottage is another cottage. This is where Bumper's neighbor, an old goat named Hornsby, lives.

One day Hornsby saw Bumper sitting in his yard drinking lemonade.

"Did you see the sunrise this morning?" asked Hornsby.

"What time did it rise?" asked Bumper.

"Five o'clock," said Hornsby.

"Then I didn't see it," Bumper answered. "At five o'clock I was sleeping."

Bumper had never seen a sunrise.

"I'll get up early tomorrow and watch it," he decided that night as he was getting ready for bed. He set his alarm for quarter to five and fell asleep.

When the alarm went off, Bumper was too tired to even open his eyes. He knocked the alarm out the window with his tail and went back to sleep.

"This will never do," said Bumper when he finally got up at ten o'clock. "I must try harder to get up and watch the sunrise."

That night Bumper placed a mousetrap on top of the clock. The next morning when the alarm went off, Bumper swatted at it and the mousetrap snapped shut on his tail.

"Yeowww!!" screamed Bumper as he jumped out of bed and pulled the mousetrap off.

Holding a bag of ice cubes on his swollen tail, Bumper went outside to wait for the sunrise.

He waited a long time. Finally his neighbor, Hornsby, called over: "Why are you sitting out there in the rain?"

"I'm waiting for the sunrise," mumbled Bumper.

"You can't see the sun rise in the rain," laughed Hornsby.

"What peculiar habits the sun has," thought Bumper.

"That night Bumper called the weather forecaster to find out if it was going to rain the next day.

"Not a drop!" promised the weather forecaster. But Bumper was not about to have his tail caught in a mousetrap again, so he decided to stay up all night. That way, when the sun rose, Bumper would be sure to see it because he'd still be awake.

He took his flashlight and a book and went outside to wait for the sunrise.

Bumper tried to read, but every time he turned on the flashlight, so many bugs swarmed around him that he couldn't see.

"I'll count stars instead," decided Bumper. But counting stars made him sleepy.

Then Bumper had a good idea. He carried his bed outside and climbed in between the covers. "Now, as soon as the sunrise is over I can go to sleep!"

The next thing Bumper knew, his neighbor, Hornsby, was shaking him and shouting: "Wake up!"

"Did I miss it?" asked Bumper. "Did I miss the sunrise?"

"By about four hours," said Hornsby. "But don't worry . . . I have a present for you."

"A present . . . for me?" said Bumper as he unwrapped it. "I wonder what it is."

"It's a picture of a sunrise," said Hornsby. "It might be the only way you'll ever get to see one."

Bumper hung the picture on the wall beside his bed, and every morning when he woke up, the first thing he saw was a beautiful sunrise.

The Frog-Jumping Contest

I<small>T WAS</small> the night before the frog-jumping contest. Bumper Tubbs's neighbor, Hornsby, was sitting on his front porch laughing and joking with his prize-winning frog, Geezer. Every year Geezer jumped farther than any other frog in the contest, and he was the favorite to win again this year.

Bumper Tubbs was sitting *alone* on *his* porch. He didn't have a frog for this year's contest. He hadn't even bothered to try to catch one. But it didn't matter . . . Geezer was unbeatable anyway. Bumper went into the house to get ready for bed.

Bumper had not been asleep for very long when he was awakened by a loud croaking noise. He stumbled to the window and looked out.

Sitting there on the edge of the swamp that bordered Bumper's yard was the biggest frog he had ever seen. "Be quiet, frog!" scolded Bumper. "I'm trying to sleep!"

"Croak!" bellowed the frog. Bumper picked up a sneaker and tossed it at the frog. But the frog jumped halfway across the swamp, and the sneaker landed with a splash far behind him.

"What a jump!" exclaimed Bumper. "I'll bet that frog can outjump that fat-head Geezer!"

Bumper took his frog net out of the closet, and with flashlight and net in hand, he went out to catch that frog.

"Here, froggy, froggy," called Bumper, as he sloshed through the swamp, getting his nightshirt all wet.

"Croak!" replied the frog.

Bumper shone his light in the direction of the sound, and, sure enough, there was the frog, sitting on a log, not ten feet away!

Swish went the net, and in an instant the frog was captured.

"Now we'll show old Hornsby and his fat-headed frog a thing or two!" Bumper chuckled, as he carried the frog into the house, tied it up in a pillowcase and placed it on the bed beside him.

In the morning Bumper was startled out of a deep sleep by a loud rumble. He sat up and looked around. "What was that?" he gasped.

"That was my stomach growling," the frog answered. "I'm starving!"

Bumper looked at the clock. "I suppose we do have time for a little breakfast before the contest," said Bumper. "What would you like?"

"Pancakes!" replied the frog. "With lots of butter and syrup!"

Bumper carried the frog to the kitchen and put him down on a chair. Then he mixed up a bowl of pancake batter and poured some on the griddle. When the pancakes were done, he stacked them on a plate and set the plate in front of the frog.

"How am I supposed to eat," the frog demanded to know, "when I'm all tied up in this pillowcase?"

"If I untie you," Bumper pointed out, "you'll run away."

"I won't run away," said the frog, his eyes bulging as he stared at the pancakes.

"Promise?" said Bumper.

"Promise!" said the frog. So Bumper untied him.

As soon as he was free, the frog grabbed a fork and began stuffing pancakes into his mouth. Bumper, meanwhile, was busy cooking some pancakes for himself. He was about to sit down to eat them when the frog shouted: "More! More pancakes, please!"

"Have these," said Bumper, handing his own plate to the frog. "I'll cook some more for me." But first Bumper had to mix up another bowlful of batter because the first bowlful was all gone.

Again Bumper was about to sit down to eat his pancakes when the frog asked for more.

"If you eat any more," said Bumper, "you won't be able to jump."

"If I don't get some more to eat," said the frog, "I won't have the strength to jump!"

So Bumper kept filling the frog's plate . . . Until finally the frog signaled — "Stop!"

"I can't eat another bite," moaned the frog.

"Good!" said Bumper. "The contest is about to begin. We'll have to hurry!"

But the frog was so stuffed with pancakes that he couldn't move.

"If you carry me," suggested the frog, "I'll probably be all right by the time we get to the contest."

"I should have known," groaned Bumper, as he picked up the frog and staggered out the door.

By the time Bumper and his frog arrived, the contest was nearly over.

"You're just in time to lose again," shouted Hornsby. "What's that you're carrying — a sack of flour?"

"This is the frog that's going to win the contest!" answered Bumper proudly.

"Geezer's going to win the contest," Hornsby assured Bumper. "See how far he jumped!"

Bumper looked into the jumping pit and there, far beyond any of the other frogs, stood Geezer.

Bumper helped *his* frog onto the jumping platform and whispered some words of encouragement. The frog tucked his legs up under his body and prepared to jump. He drew in a deep breath and wobbled to the edge of the platform. There he teetered for a moment — then burped! BURP! The frog shot straight out, as though he had been fired from a cannon.

Higher and higher! Farther and farther! Over the flag that marked Geezer's best jump went the frog, and he landed with a sickening thud right on top of poor old Geezer. Thump!! Geezer wasn't badly hurt, though, just a little sore for a few days.

When Bumper's frog was given the first-place ribbon, he smiled and said: "I owe it all to Bumper's pancakes." Everyone applauded.

Collecting Things

BUMPER TUBBS loved to collect things. He had a cart that he pushed to the dump nearly every day. At the dump he would pick through the trash, putting the things he wanted into his cart and taking them home.

When he got home, Bumper cleaned and repaired whatever he had found at the dump, then he put everything away. Some things he put in his house, other things he put into the little shed beside the house. When the house and the shed were full, Bumper left things on the porch until there was room for them inside.

The only days that Bumper didn't go to the dump were Saturday and Sunday. On Saturdays (weather permitting), Bumper took all of the things he had found at the dump and put them out on his lawn, along with a big sign that read: YARD SALE. People came from miles around to buy things that they needed at Bumper's yard sale. His prices were fair, and the merchandise was always clean and in good working order.

One day Bumper was coming back from the dump with a full load when his neighbor, Hornsby, called over to him.

"Where do you ever find all that junk?" asked Hornsby.

"This isn't junk," corrected Bumper. "It's good stuff that I find at the dump."

"It's junk!" insisted Hornsby. "It's what people throw out because it's no good anymore!"

"But *I* fix it up and make it good again," said Bumper, proudly.

"Yes," Hornsby agreed. "Then you sell it right back to the darned fools that threw it out in the first place!"

Bumper could see that it was no use discussing the matter further, so he unloaded his cart and went into his house for supper.

Bumper was eating his dessert, a slice of watermelon, when he heard a terrible racket coming from Hornsby's house.

Bumper stepped outside just in time to see Hornsby drag his refrigerator through the front door and shove it off the porch. "Crash!" it went as it landed upside-down in Hornsby's petunia bed.

"You broken-down old piece of junk!" Hornsby shouted at the refrigerator. "First thing tomorrow you're going to the dump!"

"What's wrong with it?" Bumper asked.

"It doesn't work," answered Hornsby. "It melts my ice cream and freezes my lettuce!"

"Maybe I can fix it," offered Bumper.

"It can't be fixed," said Hornsby. "Tomorrow I'm taking it to the dump, and then I'm going into town to buy a new one!"

And sure enough, when Bumper arrived at the dump the next morning, there was Hornsby's refrigerator.

That night, as Bumper pushed his fully loaded cart into his yard, he was glad that Hornsby was nowhere in sight. It wasn't until much later, when he was sitting on his front porch, catching some night air, that Bumper saw Hornsby. He was leaning on the fence that separated their yards, and he didn't look very happy.

"Priced refrigerators lately?" he asked.

"Not new ones," replied Bumper.

"Well, they're expensive," he assured Bumper. "Outrageously expensive, and not nearly as well made as they used to be."

"Did you buy one?" Bumper inquired.

"Not me," said Hornsby. "I'm no fool!"

"I have a used one that works just fine," said Bumper. "Would you like to see it?"

"It would be a waste of time," explained Hornsby. "I need one that has to fit in a certain space. It can't be too big, and I don't want one that's too small."

"Please come and see this one," urged Bumper. "It can't hurt just to look at it."

"Well, all right," said Hornsby.

Of course, Hornsby didn't know that the refrigerator he was about to look at was the very same one that he had hauled to the dump earlier that day. Bumper had brought it home, cleaned it up, and repaired it. Not only did it look like new, it worked like new, as well.

Even when he saw it, Hornsby didn't recognize his very own refrigerator. It gleamed and sparkled and hummed softly. The one he had thrown out was gray and dull and made terrible noises.

Hornsby rubbed his chin.

"Looks about the right size," he said. "But I can't be sure until I try it."

"I'll help you carry it over," said Bumper.

So the two neighbors carried the refrigerator over to Hornsby's house.

In the kitchen they set it down in front of the open space.

"So far, so good," said Hornsby, and when it slid right into the space, as if it were made for it, he cried: "Perfect!"

Hornsby was so happy. He could not thank Bumper enough.

"How much do I owe you," he asked, "for this fine refrigerator?"

"Nothing," said Bumper, and he smiled. "You've already paid me."

E   McPhail, David M.
MACP
        Bumper Tubbs 12404

E   McPhail, David M.
MACP
        Bumper Tubbs 12404